Goodnight
William

by

Alan Baker

meadowside
CHILDREN'S BOOKS

The last thing

that William expected

as he fell asleep…

… was a hole in the wall.

When the hole was big enough,

he climbed through...

...and found himself in a world of rainbows.

But then
it started
to rain,

and all the colours
were washed away,
leaving a soft pink.

After
the
rain,
tiny   and grew
blue   very quickly…
shoots
appeared

...until there was a jungle!
From out of this
jungle munched
a glump,

who was
so hungry,
he began
to eat.

As the glump ate,
he got bigger
and bigger...

...until
he just
burst, and all
that was left was
some sand and a seed.

So William put the seed
into his pocket and began
to dig deep in the sand.

Soon he had made a gigantic castle.

"Perfect!" Said William.

So he climbed to the top
of the tallest of towers,

up…

and up…

and up…

and into a snow storm.

With a loud crack
the top broke away…

...and William fell

through the hole,

landing back on his bed.

As he slept
the hole disappeared,
and all that was left
was the seed.

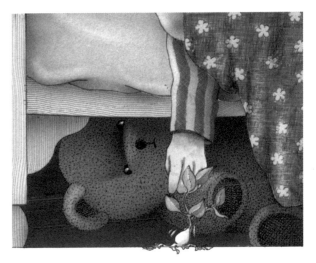

"I hope I see
the glump again,"
said William.

With love to Charlotte
AB

Meadowside Children's Books
185 Fleet Street
London
EC4A 2HS

This edition first published 2004
Text and illustrations © Alan Baker 2004
The right of Alan Baker to be identified as the author
and illustrator has been asserted by him in accordance
with the Copyright, Designs and Patents Act, 1988

A CIP catalogue record for this book is available
from the British Library
10 9 8 7 6 5 4 3 2 1
Printed in U.A.E.